CHILDREN'S THRIFT CLASSICS

Anne of Green Gables

L. M. MONTGOMERY

Abridged by Bob Blaisdell
Illustrated by Barbara Steadman

DOVER PUBLICATIONS, INC.
New York

DOVER CHILDREN'S THRIFT CLASSICS

EDITOR OF THIS VOLUME: CANDACE WARD

Copyright

Copyright © 1994 by Dover Publications, Inc.
Illustrations copyright © 1994 by Barbara Steadman.

Bibliographical Note

This Dover edition, first published in 1994, is a new abridgment of *Anne of Green Gables* (first publication, L. C. Page & Company, Boston, 1908). The illustrations and introductory Note have been specially prepared for this edition.

Library of Congress Cataloging-in-Publication Data

Blaisdell, Bob.
    Anne of Green Gables / L. M. Montgomery ; abridged by Bob Blaisdell ; illustrated by Barbara Steadman.
      p.   cm. — (Dover children's thrift classics)
    Summary: Anne, an eleven-year-old orphan, is sent by mistake to live with a lonely, middle-aged brother and sister on a Prince Edward Island farm and proceeds to make an indelible impression on everyone around her.
    ISBN-13: 978-0-486-28366-1
    ISBN-10: 0-486-28366-6 (pbk.)

    [1. Orphans—Fiction. 2. Friendship—Fiction. 3. Country life—Prince Edward Island—Fiction. 4. Prince Edward Island—Fiction.] I. Montgomery, L. M. (Lucy Maud), 1874–1942. II. Steadman, Barbara, ill. III. Title. IV. Series.
PZ7.B545An   1994
[Fic]—dc20   94–34985
                                           CIP
                                           AC

Manufactured in the United States by LSC Communications
28366618   2019
www.doverpublications.com

Note

L[ucy] M[aud] Montgomery (1874–1942) was born in Clifton, on Prince Edward Island, Canada's smallest province. Drawing on her childhood in rural Canada, Montgomery created one of the most beloved young heroines in twentieth-century children's literature: Anne of Green Gables. Like Anne, Montgomery was orphaned at a very young age. When she was two years old, her mother died and she was sent to live with her maternal grandparents on their farm. Montgomery became a teacher, but when her grandfather died she returned home to take care of her grandmother; later she went to work for a Halifax newspaper and published some of her poems and stories. What began as a serialized story for a Sunday School newspaper became her first novel, *Anne of Green Gables* (1908). The red-headed heroine was tremendously popular, and Montgomery followed with *Anne of Avonlea* (1909), *Chronicles of Avonlea* (1912), *Anne of the Island* (1915), *Anne's House of Dreams* (c. 1915), *Further Chronicles of Avonlea* (1920), *Rilla of Ingleside* (1921), *Anne of Windy Poplars* (1936) and *Anne of Ingleside* (1939). The first novel is the most popular and enduring, and generations of girls have delighted in Anne's adventures.

Contents

List of Illustrations

The good stars met in your horoscope,
Made you of spirit and fire and dew.

—BROWNING

Part I

Surprises in Avonlea

MRS. RACHEL LYNDE lived just where the Avonlea main road dipped down into a little hollow, and was crossed by a brook that had its source away back in the woods.

There are plenty of people, in Avonlea and out of it, who can attend closely to their neighbor's business by neglecting their own; but Mrs. Rachel Lynde was one of those capable creatures who can manage their own concerns and those of other folks at the same time. Mrs. Rachel found plenty of time to sit for hours at her kitchen window, knitting cotton quilts and keeping a sharp eye on the main road that crossed the hollow and wound up the steep red hill beyond. Since Avonlea was a peninsula jutting out into Canada's Gulf of St. Lawrence, with water on two sides of it, anybody who went out of it or into it had to pass over the hill road and pass by Mrs. Rachel's all-seeing eye.

She was sitting there one afternoon in early June when Matthew Cuthbert, the shyest man alive and who hated to have to go among

1

strangers or to any place where he might have to talk, came calmly driving his horse and buggy over the hollow and up the hill.

She said to herself, "I'll just step over to Green Gables and find out from Marilla where he's gone and why. He doesn't generally go to town this time of year and he *never* visits."

The Cuthberts, brother and sister, lived up the road from Lynde's Hollow. Green Gables was built at the furthest edge of Matthew's father's cleared land and there it was to this day, barely visible from the main road along which all the other Avonlea houses were situated.

Mrs. Rachel stepped out of the lane and into the backyard of Green Gables. She rapped at the kitchen door and stepped in when called out to do so. There sat Marilla Cuthbert knitting, and the table behind her was laid for supper—for three people.

Mrs. Rachel was almost dizzy with this mystery about quiet, unmysterious Green Gables.

Marilla was a tall, thin woman; her dark hair showed some gray streaks and was always twisted up in a hard little knot behind with two hairpins stuck through it. "Matthew went to Bright River," explained Marilla to her friend. "We're getting a little boy from an orphan asylum in Nova Scotia and he's coming on the train tonight."

If Marilla had said that Matthew had gone to Bright River to meet a kangaroo from Australia, Mrs. Rachel could not have been more astonished.

"Are you serious?" she demanded.

"Yes, of course," said Marilla, as if getting boys from orphan asylums in Nova Scotia were part of the usual spring work on any Avonlea farm.

"What on earth put such a notion into your head?"

"Well, we've been thinking about it for some time—all winter, in fact," said Marilla. "Mrs. Alexander Spencer was up here one day before Christmas and she said she was going to get a little girl from the asylum over in Hopetown in the spring. So Matthew and I have talked it over off and on ever since. Matthew is getting up in years, you know—he's sixty—and he isn't so spry as he once was. His heart troubles him a good deal. And you know how desperate hard it's got to be to get hired help. So in the end we decided to ask Mrs. Spencer to pick us out one when she went over to get her little girl. We sent word by Richard Spencer's folks to bring us a smart boy of about ten or eleven—old enough to be of some use in doing chores right off and young enough to be trained up proper. We mean to give him a good home and schooling."

"Well, Marilla," said Mrs. Rachel, "I'll just tell you plain that I think you're doing a mighty foolish thing—a risky thing, that's what. You're bringing a strange child into your house and home and you don't know a single thing about him nor how he's likely to turn out. If you had asked my advice in the matter—which you didn't do, Marilla—I'd have said for mercy's sake not to think of such a thing, that's what."

"I don't deny there's something in what you say, Rachel," returned Marilla. "I've had some doubts myself. But Matthew was terribly set on it, so I gave in. As for the risk, there's risks in pretty near everything a body does in this world. I'd never dream of taking a girl to bring up. I wonder at Mrs. Alexander for doing it."

When Mrs. Rachel set out then to spread the news, she said to herself, "It seems odd to think of a child at Green Gables. There's never been one there."

Matthew Cuthbert enjoyed the drive to Bright River except during the moments when he met women and had to nod to them—on Prince Edward Island you are supposed to nod to everyone you meet on the road whether you know them or not.

Matthew dreaded all women except Marilla and Mrs. Rachel; he had an uncomfortable feeling that women were secretly laughing at him. He may have been right; he was an odd-looking man, with a clumsy manner and long, gray hair that touched his stooping shoulders, and a full, soft brown beard which he had worn ever since he was twenty.

When he reached Bright River there was no sign of any train; he thought he was too early. The long platform at the station was almost deserted; the only living creature in sight was a girl who was sitting on a pile of shingles at the far end.

Matthew found the stationmaster locking up the ticket office before going home to supper, and asked him if the five-thirty train would soon be along.

"The five-thirty train has been in and gone half an hour ago," said the man. "But there was a passenger dropped off for you—a little girl. She's sitting out there on the shingles."

"I'm not expecting a girl," said Matthew. "It's a boy I've come for. He should be here."

"Guess there's some mistake," said the stationmaster. "Mrs. Spencer came off the train with that girl and gave her into my care. She said you and your sister were adopting her from an orphan asylum."

Poor Matthew was left to do that which was harder for him than pulling a lion's beard—walk up to a girl—a strange girl—an orphan girl—and demand of her why she wasn't a boy.

She was a child of about eleven, clothed in a very short, very tight, very ugly yellowish dress. She wore a faded brown sailor hat and beneath the hat, extending down her back, were two braids of very thick red hair. Her face was small, white and thin, also quite freckled; her mouth was large and so were her gray eyes, which looked green in some lights and moods and gray in others. Those big eyes were full of spirit and liveliness.

*The only living creature in sight was a girl who was
sitting on a pile of shingles.*

Shy Matthew Cuthbert was ridiculously afraid of this stray woman-child.

As soon as the girl was sure that he was coming to her she stood up, grasping with one thin hand the handle of a shabby, old-fashioned bag; the other hand she held out to him.

"I suppose you are Mr. Matthew Cuthbert of Green Gables?" she said in a sweet voice. "I'm very glad to see you. I was beginning to be afraid you weren't coming for me and I was imagining all the things that might have happened to prevent you. I had made up my mind that if you didn't come for me tonight I'd go down the track to that big wild cherry tree at the bend, and climb up into it to stay all night. I wouldn't be a bit afraid, and it would be lovely to sleep in a wild cherry tree all white with bloom in the moonshine, don't you think? And I was quite sure you would come for me in the morning, if you didn't tonight."

Matthew had taken her scrawny little hand in his; then and there he decided what to do. He could not tell this child with the glowing eyes that there had been a mistake; he would take her home and let Marilla do that.

"I'm sorry I was late," he said. "Come along. The horse is over in the yard. Give me your bag."

"Oh, I can carry it," said the child. "It isn't heavy. I've got all my worldly goods in it, but it isn't heavy. And if it isn't carried in just a certain way the handle pulls out—so I'd better keep it because I know the exact knack of it. We've got to drive a long piece, haven't we? I'm glad because I love driving. Oh, it seems so wonderful that I'm going to live with you and belong to you. I've never belonged to anybody—not really. But the asylum was the worst. I don't suppose you ever were an orphan in an asylum, so you can't possibly understand what it is like. It's worse than anything you can imagine. They were good, you know—the asylum people. But there is so little scope for the imagination in an asylum— only just in the other orphans. It *was* pretty interesting to imagine things about them—to imagine that perhaps the girl who sat next to you was really the daughter of a rich man, who had been stolen away from her parents as a baby by a cruel nurse. I used to lie awake at nights and imagine things like that, because I didn't have time in the day. I guess that's why I'm so thin—I am dreadful thin, ain't I? I do love to imagine I'm nice and plump, with dimples in my elbows."

With this Matthew's companion stopped talking, partly because she was out of breath and partly because they had reached the buggy. Not another word did she say until they had left the village and were driving down a steep little hill. She put out her hand and broke off a branch of wild plum that brushed against the side of the buggy.

"What did that tree make you think of?" she asked.

"Well now, I dunno," said Matthew.

"Why, a bride, of course—a bride all in white with a lovely misty veil. I don't ever expect to be a bride myself. I'm so homely nobody will ever want to marry me. But I do hope that some day I shall have a white dress. That is my highest ideal of earthly bliss. I just love pretty clothes. And I've never had a pretty dress in my life that I can remember. But then I can imagine that I'm dressed gorgeously. This morning when I left the asylum I felt so ashamed because I had to wear this horrid old dress. When we got on the train I felt as if everybody must be looking at me and pitying me. But I just went to work and imagined that I had on the most beautiful pale blue silk dress and a big hat with nodding plumes, and a gold watch, and fine gloves and boots. I felt cheered up right away and I enjoyed my trip to Prince Edward Island with all my might. Oh, there are a lot more cherry trees all in bloom! This island is the bloomiest place. I just love it already, and I'm so glad I'm going to live here. I've always heard that Prince Edward Island was the prettiest place in the world, and I used to imagine I was living here, but I never really expected I would. It's delightful when your imaginations come true, isn't it?—What makes the roads here so red?"

"Well now, I dunno," said Matthew.

"Well, that is one of the things to find out sometime. Isn't it splendid to think of all the things there are to find out about? It just makes me feel glad to be alive—it's such an interesting world. It wouldn't be half so interesting if we knew all about everything, would it? There'd be no scope for imagination then, would there? But am I talking too much? People are always telling me I do. Would you rather I didn't talk? If you say so, I'll stop. I *can* stop when I make up my mind to it, although it's difficult."

Matthew, much to his own surprise, was enjoying himself. Although he found it rather difficult to keep up with her he thought that he "kind of liked her chatter." So he said, "Oh, you can talk as much as you like. I don't mind."

"Oh, I'm so glad. I know you and I are going to get along together fine. It's such a relief to talk when one wants to and not be told that children should be seen and not heard. People laugh at me because I use big words. But if you have big ideas you have to use big words to express them, haven't you?"

"Well now, that seems reasonable," said Matthew.

"Mrs. Spencer said your place was named Green Gables. I asked her all about it. And she said there were trees all around it. I was gladder than ever. I just love trees. Is there a brook near Green Gables? I forgot to ask Mrs. Spencer that."

"Well now, yes, there's one right below the house."

"Fancy! It's always been one of my dreams to

live near a brook. I never expected I would though. Dreams don't often come true, do they? Wouldn't it be nice if they did? But just now I feel pretty nearly perfectly happy. I can't feel exactly perfectly happy because—well, what color would you call this?"

She twitched one of her long braids over her thin shoulder and held it before Matthew's eyes.

"It's red, ain't it?" he said.

"Yes, it's red," she said. "Now you see why I can't be perfectly happy. Nobody could who had red hair. I don't mind the other things so much— the freckles and the green eyes and my skinniness. I can imagine them away, but I *cannot* imagine that red hair away. It will be my lifetime sorrow. Have you ever imagined what it must feel like to be divinely beautiful?"

"Well now, no, I haven't," confessed Matthew.

"I have, often. Which would you rather be if you had the choice—divinely beautiful or dazzlingly clever or angelically good?"

"Well now, I—I don't know exactly."

"Neither do I. I can never decide. But it doesn't make much real difference for it isn't likely I'll ever be either."

After they passed through Newbridge the girl fell into silence as she gazed at the beautiful trees and at the sunset.

"I guess you're feeling pretty tired and hungry," said Matthew at last. "But we haven't very far to go now—only another mile."

"I'm glad and I'm sorry. I'm sorry because this drive has been so pleasant and I'm always sorry when pleasant things end. But I'm glad to think of getting home. You see, I've never had a real home since I can remember."

"We're pretty near home now," said Matthew. "That's Green Gables over——"

"Oh, don't tell me. Let me guess. I'm sure I'll guess right."

They were on the crest of a hill. The sun had set some time since, but the landscape was still clear in the afterlight. Below was a little valley and beyond a long, gently rising slope with farmsteads scattered along it. From one to another the girl's eyes darted. At last she fixed on a farmstead away to the left, far back from the road.

"That's it, isn't it?" she said, pointing.

"Well now, you've guessed it!"

"Just as soon as I saw it I felt I was home. Oh, it seems I must be in a dream." With a sigh she fell back into silence. Matthew felt glad that it would be Marilla and not he who would have to tell this orphan that the home she longed for was not to be hers after all. By the time they arrived at the house Matthew was shrinking from the approaching revelation. It was not of Marilla or himself he was thinking or of the trouble this mistake was probably going to make for them, but of the child's disappointment.

The yard was quite dark as they turned into it.

"Listen to the trees talking in their sleep," she whispered, as he lifted her down from the buggy to the ground. "What nice dreams they must have!"

Then, holding tightly to the bag which contained "all her worldly goods," she followed him into the house.

Marilla came forward as Matthew opened the door. But when her eyes fell on the odd little figure in the stiff, ugly dress, with the long braids of red hair and the eager, bright eyes, she stopped short in amazement. "Matthew Cuthbert," she exclaimed. "Where is the boy?"

"There wasn't any boy," said Matthew. "There was only her."

He nodded at the child, remembering that he had never even asked her name.

"No boy! But there *must* have been a boy," insisted Marilla. "We sent word for Mrs. Spencer to bring a boy."

"Well, she didn't. She brought *her*. I asked the stationmaster. And I had to bring her home. She couldn't be left there."

"Well, this is a pretty piece of business!" said Marilla.

During this talk the child remained silent, her eyes going from one to the other. Suddenly she seemed to grasp the full meaning of what had been said.

"You don't want me!" she cried. "You don't want me because I'm not a boy! I might have expected it. Nobody ever did want me. I might have known it was all too beautiful to last. I might have known nobody really did want me. Oh, what shall I do? I'm going to burst into tears!"

Burst into tears she did. Marilla and Matthew looked at each other. Neither of them knew what to say or do. Finally Marilla said, "Well, well, there's no need to cry so about it."

"Yes, there *is* need! *You* would cry, too, if you were an orphan and had come to a place you thought was going to be home and found that they didn't want you because you weren't a boy. Oh, this is the most *tragical* thing that ever happened to me!"

Marilla smiled a little and said, "Well, don't cry any more. We're not going to turn you out-of-doors tonight. You'll have to stay here until we find out what happened. What's your name?"

The child hesitated for a moment.

"Will you please call me Cordelia?" she said.

"*Call* you Cordelia! Is that your name?"

"No-o-o, it's not exactly my name, but I would love to be called Cordelia. It's such a perfectly elegant name."

"I don't know what on earth you mean. If Cordelia isn't your name, what is?"

"Anne Shirley," the child said, "but oh, do call me Cordelia. Anne is such an unromantic name."

"Unromantic fiddlesticks!" said Marilla. "Anne is a real good plain sensible name. You've no need to be ashamed of it."

"Oh, I'm not ashamed of it," explained Anne, "only I like Cordelia better. But if you call me Anne, please call me Anne spelled with an *e.*"

"What difference does it make how it's spelled?" asked Marilla with another little smile as she picked up the teapot.

"Oh, it makes *such* a difference. It *looks* so much nicer. When you hear your name pronounced can't you always see it in your mind, just as if it was printed out? I can; and A-n-n looks dreadful, but A-n-n-e looks so much more distinguished. If you'll only call me Anne spelled with an *e* I shall try to reconcile myself to not being Cordelia."

"Very well, Anne spelled with an *e,* can you tell us how this mistake came to be made? Were there no boys at the asylum?"

"Oh, yes, there was an abundance. But Mrs. Spencer said distinctly that you wanted a girl about eleven years old. You don't know how delighted I was. I couldn't sleep all last night for joy."

When Matthew had gone out to put the horse away, Marilla asked, "Did Mrs. Spencer bring anybody over besides you?"

"She brought Lily Jones for herself. Lily is only five years old and she is very beautiful. If I was beautiful and had nut-brown hair would you keep me?"

"No, we want a boy to help Matthew on the farm. A girl would be of no use to us."

Matthew soon came back and they sat down to supper. But Anne could not eat.

"You're not eating anything," said Marilla.

"I can't. I'm in the depths of despair. Can you eat when you are in the depths of despair?"

"I've never been in the depths of despair, so I can't say," responded Marilla.

"Weren't you? Well, did you ever try to *imagine* you were in the depths of despair?"

"No, I didn't."

"Then I don't think you can understand what it's like. I do hope you won't be offended because I can't eat. Everything is extremely nice, but still I cannot eat."

"I guess she's tired," said Matthew. "Best put her to bed, Marilla."

Marilla lighted a candle and told Anne to follow her and led the child to the east gable room.

After Anne changed into her nightgown and got into bed, Marilla said, "Good night."

"How can you call it a *good* night when you know it must be the very worst night I've ever had?" Anne said.

Marilla went slowly down to the kitchen, where Matthew was smoking—a sure sign he was upset.

"Well, this a pretty kettle of fish," she said. "This is what comes of sending word instead of going ourselves. One of us will have to drive over and see Mrs. Spencer tomorrow, that's certain. This girl will have to be sent back to the asylum."

"Yes, I suppose so," said Matthew.

"You suppose so! Don't you know it?"

"Well now, she's a real nice little thing, Marilla. It's kind of a pity to send her back when she's so set on staying here."

"Matthew Cuthbert, you don't mean to say you think we ought to keep her!"

"Well now, no, I suppose not—not exactly," stammered Matthew. "I suppose—we could hardly be expected to keep her."

"I should say not. What good would she be to us?"

"We might be some good to her," said Matthew.

"Matthew Cuthbert, I believe that child has bewitched you! I can see as plain as plain that you want to keep her."

"Well now, she's a real interesting little thing," said Matthew. "You should have heard her talk coming from the station."

"Oh, she can talk fast enough. I saw that at once. It's nothing in her favor, either. I don't like children who have so much to say. I don't want an orphan girl and if I did she isn't the style I'd pick out. There's something I don't understand about her. No, she's got to be sent back to where she came from."

Upstairs, in the east gable, a lonely, heart-hungry child cried herself to sleep.

Part II

Anne Finds a Home

IT WAS BROAD daylight when Anne awoke. For a moment she could not remember where she was. Then she did remember! This was Green Gables and they didn't want her because she wasn't a boy!

But it was morning and there was a cherry tree in full bloom outside of her window. With a bound she was out of bed and across the floor. Anne dropped on her knees and gazed out the open window into the June morning. She had looked on many unlovely places in her life, poor child; but this was as lovely as anything she had ever dreamed.

Marilla came in unheard by the small dreamer.

"It's time you were dressed," she said.

Anne stood up and said, "Oh, isn't it wonderful? I mean everything, the garden and the orchard and the brook and the woods, the whole big dear world. Don't you feel as if you just loved the world on a morning like this? I'm not in the depths of despair this morning. I never can be in the morning. Isn't it a splendid thing that there

*Anne dropped on her knees and gazed out the open
window into the June morning.*

are mornings? But I feel very sad. I've just been imagining that it was really me you wanted after all and that I was to stay here for ever and ever. But the worst of imagining things is that the time comes when you have to stop and that hurts."

"You'd better get dressed and come downstairs and never mind your imaginings," said Marilla.

When Anne arrived at the table shortly after, she said, "I'm so glad it's a sunshiny morning. But I like rainy mornings real well, too. All sorts of mornings are interesting, don't you think? You don't know what's going to happen to you through the day and there's so much scope for imagination."

"For pity's sake hold your tongue," said Marilla. "You talk entirely too much for a little girl. What's to be done with you I don't know. Matthew is a most ridiculous man."

"I think he's lovely," said Anne. "He is so very nice. He didn't mind how much I talked—he seemed to like it. I felt that he was a kindred spirit as soon as ever I saw him."

"You're both strange enough, if that's what you mean by kindred spirits," said Marilla. "After you've finished the dishes go upstairs and make your bed."

When Anne was done with those chores Marilla told her that she might go out-of-doors and amuse herself until lunchtime.

Anne flew to the door and then stopped, wheeled about, came back and sat down by the table.

"What's the matter now?" demanded Marilla.

"I don't dare go out," said Anne. "If I can't stay here there is no use in my loving Green Gables. I want to go out so much—everything seems to be calling to me, 'Anne, Anne, come out to us. Anne, Anne, we want a playmate'—but I'd better not. There is no use in loving things if you have to be torn from them, is there? And it's *so* hard to keep from loving things, isn't it?"

Marilla, beating a retreat down into the cellar to get some potatoes, muttered, "I never in all my life saw or heard anything to equal her. She *is* kind of interesting, as Matthew says. I can feel already that I'm wondering what on earth she'll say next. She'll be casting a spell over me, too. She's cast it over Matthew."

After lunch Matthew hitched the horse into the buggy and Marilla and Anne set off for Mrs. Spencer's house.

"Do you know," said Anne to Marilla, "I've made up my mind to enjoy this drive. It's been my experience that you can nearly always enjoy things if you make up your mind that you will. I am not going to think about going back to the asylum, I'm just going to think about the drive."

"As you're evidently bent on talking," said Marilla, "you might as well talk to some purpose by telling me what you know about yourself. Where were you born and how old are you?"

"I was eleven last March," said Anne. "And I was born in Bolingbroke, Nova Scotia. My father's name was Walter Shirley and he was a teacher in in the Bolingbroke High School. My mother's name was Bertha Shirley. She was a teacher in the high school, too, but when she married father she gave up teaching. She died of fever when I was just three months old. I do wish she'd lived long enough for me to remember calling her mother. And father died four days afterwards from fever, too. That left me an orphan and folks were at their wits' end. You see, nobody wanted me even then. It seems to be my fate. Finally Mrs. Thomas said she'd take me, though she was poor and had a drunken husband. I lived with them until I was eight years old. I helped look after the Thomas children—there were four of them younger than me. Then Mr. Thomas was killed falling under a train and his mother offered to take Mrs. Thomas and the children, but she didn't want me. Then Mrs. Hammond from up the river came down and said she'd take me, seeing I was handy with children. It was a very lonesome place. I lived up river with Mrs. Hammond over two years, and then Mr. Hammond died and Mrs. Hammond divided her children among her relatives and went to the States. I had to go to the asylum in Hopeton, because nobody would take me. I was there four months until Mrs. Spencer came."

"Did you ever go to school?" asked Marilla.

"Not a great deal. But I can read pretty well and I know ever so many pieces of poetry off by heart. Don't you just love poetry that gives you a crinkly feeling up and down your back?"

"Were those women," interrupted Marilla, "that Mrs. Thomas and Mrs. Hammond, were they good to you?"

"Oh, they *meant* to be—I know they meant to be just as good and kind as possible."

Marilla asked no more questions. Anne watched the shore as they rode along, and Marilla guided the horse absent-mindedly while she pondered deeply. Pity was suddenly stirring in her heart for the child. What a starved, unloved life she had had—a life of drudgery and poverty and neglect. What if she, Marilla, should let her stay? Matthew was already set on it; and the child seemed a nice, teachable little thing.

"She's got too much to say," thought Marilla, "but she might be trained out of that."

Soon Marilla and Anne arrived at Mrs. Spencer's house. "The fact is, Mrs. Spencer," said Marilla, "there's been a strange mistake somewhere, and I've come over to see where it is. We sent word, Matthew and I, for you to bring us a boy from the asylum. We told your brother Robert to tell you we wanted a boy ten or eleven years old."

"I'm dreadful sorry," said Mrs. Spencer. "It is too bad; but it certainly wasn't my fault. Robert sent his daughter Nancy, and she is a terribly flighty thing. Nancy told us you wanted a girl."

"It was our own fault," said Marilla. "We should not have left an important message to be passed along by word of mouth. Anyhow, the mistake has been made and the only thing to do now is to set it right. I suppose the asylum will take her back, won't they?"

"I suppose so," said Mrs. Spencer, "but I don't think it will be necessary to send her back. Mrs. Peter Blewett was saying to me how much she wished she'd sent for a little girl to help her. Mrs. Peter has a large family, you know, and she finds it hard to get help. Anne will be the very girl for her."

Marilla knew Mrs. Peter Blewett to be mean and stingy, with a family of rude, quarrelsome children. Marilla felt bad at the idea of handing Anne over to that woman.

By the worse bad luck Mrs. Blewett came walking past Mrs. Spencer's house that very moment. Mrs. Spencer called out to her to come in. Mrs. Spencer explained to her about the confusion over the Cuthberts' request for an orphan child, and how here was a spare girl just as Mrs. Blewett needed.

Mrs. Blewett looked over Anne from head to foot.

"Yes, I suppose I might as well take her off your hands, Miss Cuthbert. The baby's awful fussy, and I'm clear worn out attending to him. If you like I can take her right along home now."

Marilla looked at Anne and softened at sight of the child's pale face with its looks of silent misery. "Well, I don't know," Marilla said slowly.

"I didn't say we wouldn't keep her. In fact, I may say that Matthew is disposed to keep her. I just came over to find out how the mistake had occurred. I think I'd better take her home and talk it over with Matthew."

During Marilla's speech a bright look dawned on Anne's face.

As soon as Mrs. Spencer and Mrs. Blewett went out of the room for a recipe, Anne sprang up and flew across the room to Marilla.

"Oh, Miss Cuthbert, did you really say that perhaps you would let me stay at Green Gables? Did you really say it? Or did I only imagine that you did?"

"Yes, you did hear me say just that and no more. It isn't decided yet and perhaps we will conclude to let Mrs. Blewett take you after all. She certainly needs you much more than I do."

"I'd rather go back to the asylum than go to live with her," said Anne. "I'll try to do and be anything you want me, if you'll only keep me."

When they arrived back at Green Gables that evening, Matthew met them in the lane. When he and Marilla were alone later she briefly told him Anne's history and about Mrs. Blewett's wish to take Anne.

"I wouldn't give a dog to that Blewett woman," said Matthew.

"I don't fancy her myself," admitted Marilla, "but it's either that or keeping her ourselves. And since you seem to want her, I suppose I'm willing—or have to be. I've been thinking over the idea until I've got kind of used to it. It seems a sort of duty. So far as I'm concerned, Matthew, she may stay."

Matthew's face glowed.

"Well now, I reckoned you'd come to see it in that light, Marilla," he said. "She's such an interesting little thing."

"It'd be more to the point if you could say she was a useful little thing," said Marilla, "but I'll make it my business to see she's trained to be that. And mind, Matthew, you're not to go interfering with my methods. Perhaps an old maid doesn't know much about bringing up a child, but I guess she knows more than an old bachelor like you."

"There, there, Marilla, you can have your own way," said Matthew. "Only I kind of think she's one of the sort you can do anything with if you only get her to love you."

When Marilla took Anne up to bed that night she said, "You must say your prayers while you are under my roof, Anne."

"Why, of course, if you want me to," said Anne. "But you'll have to tell me what to do and say for this once. I never said any prayers."

"You must kneel down," said Marilla.

"Well, I'm ready. What am I to say?"

"You're old enough to pray for yourself, Anne," she said. "Just thank God for your blessings and ask Him humbly for the things you want."

"Well, I'll do my best," promised Anne. "Gracious heavenly Father, I thank Thee for the White Way of Delight we drove along today and the Lake of Shining Waters pond and Bonny the geranium and the Snow Queen cherry tree. I'm really extremely grateful for them. As for the things I want, they're so numerous that it would take a great deal of time to name them all, so I will only mention the two most important. Please let me stay at Green Gables; and please let me be good-looking when I grow up. I remain, Yours respectfully, Anne Shirley.—There," she said getting up, "did I do it all right? I should have said 'Amen' in place of 'yours respectfully,' shouldn't I? Do you suppose it will make any difference?"

"I—I don't suppose it will," said Marilla. "Go to sleep now like a good child. Good night."

When Marilla went down to the kitchen, she found Matthew there and scolded him. "Matthew Cuthbert, it's about time somebody adopted that child and taught her something. Will you believe that she never said a prayer in her life till tonight? I foresee that I shall have my hands full. Well, well, we can't get through this world without our share of trouble. I've had a pretty easy life of it so far, but my time has come at last and I suppose I'll just have to make the best of it."

Marilla did not tell Anne that she was to stay at Green Gables until the next afternoon. When Anne had finished washing the lunch dishes she suddenly confronted Marilla. Her thin little body trembled from head to foot; she clasped her hands and said, "Oh, please, Miss Cuthbert, won't you tell me if you are going to send me away or not? I've tried to be patient all the morning, but I really feel that I cannot bear not knowing any longer. Please tell me."

"Well," said Marilla, "I suppose I might as well tell you. Matthew and I have decided to keep you—that is, if you will try to be a good little girl and show yourself grateful. Why, child, whatever is the matter?"

"I'm crying," said Anne, surprised. "I can't think why. I'm glad as can be. I'm so happy. I'll try to be so good. But can you tell me why I'm crying?"

"I suppose it's because you're all excited and worked up," said Marilla. "Sit down on that chair and try to calm yourself. I'm afraid you both cry and laugh far too easily. Yes, you can stay here and we will try to do right by you."

"What am I to call you?" asked Anne. "Shall I always say Miss Cuthbert? Can I call you Aunt Marilla?"

"No; you'll call me just plain Marilla."

"I'd love to call you Aunt Marilla. I've never had an aunt or any relation at all. Can't I call you Aunt Marilla?"

"No. I'm not your aunt and I don't believe in calling people names that don't belong to them."

"But we could imagine you were my aunt."

"I couldn't," said Marilla.

"Do you never imagine things different from what they really are?" asked Anne.

"No."

"Oh!" said Anne. "Oh, Marilla, how much you miss!"

"I don't believe in imagining things different from what they really are."

Marilla made Anne learn a prayer that afternoon, but because the girl would not stop talking to her, asking questions, marvelling over blossoms and bees, Marilla sent her up to her room to learn it. Anne memorized the prayer in almost no time and began to imagine her room was like one in a palace.

"I can see my reflection in that splendid big mirror hanging on the wall," she said to herself. "I am tall and regal, clothed in a gown of trailing white lace, with a pearl cross on my breast and pearls in my hair. My hair is of midnight darkness and my skin is a clear ivory. My name is the Lady Cordelia Fitzgerald. No, it isn't—I can't make *that* seem real."

She danced up to the little looking-glass and peered into it. Her freckled face and gray eyes peered back at her.

"You're only Anne of Green Gables," she said, "and I see you, just as you are looking now, whenever I try to imagine I'm the Lady Cordelia. But it's a million times nicer to be Anne of Green Gables than Anne of nowhere in particular, isn't it?"

She bent forward, kissed her reflection, and then went and looked out the open window.

Part III

Tempests in Teapots

ANNE HAD BEEN two weeks at Green Gables before Mrs. Rachel Lynde arrived to inspect her. When Mrs. Lynde came over that afternoon for tea, Anne was out in the orchard.

Mrs. Rachel said to Marilla, "I've been hearing some surprising things about you and Matthew. Couldn't you have sent her back?"

"I suppose we could, but we decided not to. The house seems a different place already. She's a real bright little thing. I'll call her in."

Anne came running, her face sparkling; but, embarrassed at finding herself in the presence of a stranger, she stopped just inside the door. She certainly was an odd-looking creature in the short, cheap dress she had worn from the asylum, and with her thin, long legs. Her freckles were more obvious than ever; the wind had ruffled her hair, and it looked redder than ever.

"Well, they didn't pick you for your looks, that's sure and certain," was Mrs. Rachel Lynde's first comment. "She's terrible skinny and homely, Marilla. Come here, child, and let me have a look at you. Did any one ever see such freckles? And hair as red as carrots! Come here, child, I say."

Anne "came there," but not exactly as Mrs. Rachel expected. With one bound she crossed the kitchen floor and stood before Mrs. Rachel, her face red with anger, her lips quivering, and her whole form trembling. "I hate you," she cried, stamping her foot on the floor. "I hate you—I hate you—I hate you——" a louder stamp with each declaration. "How dare you call me skinny and ugly? How dare you say I'm freckled and redheaded? You are a rude, impolite, unfeeling woman!"

"Anne!" said Marilla.

But Anne continued to face Mrs. Rachel, head up, eyes blazing. "How dare you say such things about me? How would you like to have such things said about you? How would you like to be told that you are fat and clumsy and probably hadn't a spark of imagination in you? I don't care if I hurt your feelings by saying so! I hope I hurt them. You have hurt mine worse than they were ever hurt before. And I'll never forgive you for it, never, never!"

Stamp! Stamp!

"Did anybody ever see such a temper?" exclaimed the horrified Mrs. Rachel.

"Anne, go to your room and stay there until I come up," said Marilla.

Anne, bursting into tears, rushed to the hall

With one bound she crossed the kitchen floor and stood before Mrs. Rachel, her face red with anger, her lips quivering, and her whole form trembling.

door, slammed it and fled through the hall and up the stairs like a whirlwind.

"Well, I don't envy you your job bringing *that* up, Marilla," said Mrs. Rachel.

"You shouldn't have teased her about her looks, Rachel," said Marilla. "I'm not trying to excuse her. She's been very naughty and I'll have to give her a talking to about it. But we must make allowances for her. She's never been taught what is right. And you *were* too hard on her, Rachel."

"Well," said Rachel, getting up and looking offended, "I see that I'll have to be very careful what I say after this, Marilla, since the fine feelings of orphans, brought from goodness knows where, have to be considered before anything else. Her temper matches her hair, I guess. Well, good evening, Marilla."

After Mrs. Rachel waddled off toward home, Marilla went upstairs. She found Anne face downward on her bed, crying.

"Anne," she said. "Get off that bed this minute and listen to what I have to say to you."

Anne squirmed off the bed and sat on a chair beside it.

"This is a nice way to behave, Anne! Aren't you ashamed of yourself?"

"She hadn't any right to call me ugly and redheaded," said Anne.

"You hadn't any right to fly into such a fury and talk the way you did to her, Anne. I was ashamed of you—thoroughly ashamed of you. I wanted you to behave nicely to Mrs. Lynde, and instead you have disgraced me. I'm sure I don't know why you should lose your temper like that just because Mrs. Lynde said you were redhaired and homely. You say it yourself often enough."

"Oh, but there's such a difference between saying a thing yourself and hearing other people say it," sobbed Anne. "You may know a thing is so, but you can't help hoping other people don't quite think it is. Just imagine how you would feel if somebody told you to your face that you were skinny and ugly," pleaded Anne.

"I don't say that I think Mrs. Lynde was exactly right in saying what she did to you, Anne. Rachel is too outspoken. But that is no excuse for such behavior on your part. You were rude and saucy and you must go to her and tell her you are very sorry for your bad temper and ask her to forgive you."

"I can never do that," said Anne. "You can punish me in any way you like, Marilla. You can shut me up in a dark, damp dungeon inhabited by snakes and toads and feed me only on bread and water and I shall not complain. But I cannot ask Mrs. Lynde to forgive me."

"We're not in the habit of shutting people up in dark, damp dungeons," said Marilla, "especially as they're rather scarce in Avonlea. But apologize to Mrs. Lynde you must and shall and you'll stay here in your room until you can tell me you're willing to do it."

"I shall have to stay here forever then," said Anne, "because I can't tell Mrs. Lynde I'm sorry I said those things to her. I'm sorry I've vexed you; but I'm glad I told her just what I did.".

The next evening, while Marilla was off in a far pasture leading back the cows, Matthew came by Anne's room to see if he could encourage her to apologize. "Well now, Anne, don't you think you'd better do it and have it over with? It'll have to be done sooner or later, you know, for Marilla's a dreadful determined woman. Do it right off, I say, and have it over."

"I suppose I could apologize to oblige you," said Anne. "It would be true enough to say I am sorry, because I am sorry now. I wasn't a bit sorry last night. But this morning I wasn't in a temper any more. I felt so ashamed of myself. But I just couldn't think of going and telling Mrs. Lynde so. I made up my mind I'd stay shut up here forever rather than do that. But still—if you really want me to——"

"Well now, of course I do. It's terrible lonesome downstairs without you."

When Marilla brought Anne to Mrs. Rachel Lynde's that evening, Anne went down on her knees before the astonished Mrs. Rachel and held out her hands.

"Oh, Mrs. Lynde, I am so extremely sorry. I could never express all my sorrow, no, not if I used up a whole dictionary. I behaved terribly to you—and I've disgraced my dear friends, Matthew and Marilla, who have let me stay at Green Gables although I'm not a boy. It was very wicked of me to fly into a temper because you told me the truth. It was the truth; every word you said was true. My hair is red and I'm freckled and skinny and ugly. What I said to you was true, too, but I shouldn't have said it. Oh, Mrs. Lynde, please, please, forgive me."

"There, there, get up, child," said Mrs. Lynde. "Of course I forgive you. I guess I was a little too hard on you, anyway. It can't be denied your hair is terrible red; but I knew a girl once whose hair was every mite as red as yours when she was young, but when she grew up it darkened to a real handsome auburn. I wouldn't be a mite surprised if yours did, too."

"Oh, Mrs. Lynde," said Anne. "You have given me a hope. I shall always feel that you are a benefactor. Oh, I could endure anything if I only thought my hair would be a handsome auburn when I grew up."

When Marilla and Anne were returning home, Anne said, "I apologized pretty well, didn't I? I thought since I had to do it I might as well do it thoroughly. I have no hard feelings against Mrs. Lynde now. It gives you a lovely, comfortable feeling to apologize and be forgiven, doesn't it? Aren't the stars bright tonight? If you could live in a star, which one would you pick? I'd like that lovely clear big one away over there above that dark hill."

"Anne, do hold your tongue," said Marilla, worn out trying to follow Anne's thoughts.

Anne said no more until they turned into their own lane. She suddenly came close to Marilla and slipped her hand into the older woman's hard palm.

"It's lovely to be going home and know it's home," she said. "I love Green Gables already, and I never loved any place before. Oh, Marilla, I'm so happy."

Something warm and pleasant welled up in Marilla's heart at the touch of that thin little hand in her own.

A week later, Marilla announced that she and Anne would go over to the Barrys' house, and that Anne could get acquainted with Diana, a girl Anne's age.

"Oh, Marilla," said Anne, "I'm frightened. What if she doesn't like me! It would be the most tragical disappointment of my life."

"Now, don't get into a fluster. And I do wish you wouldn't use such long words. It sounds so funny in a little girl. I guess Diana'll like you well enough.—For pity's sake, if you aren't actually trembling!"

"Oh, Marilla, you'd be excited, too, if you were going to meet a little girl you hoped to be your bosom friend and whose mother mightn't like you."

They went over to Orchard Slope by the

short cut across the brook and up the hill. Mrs. Barry was a tall, black-eyed, black-haired woman. Diana was a very pretty little girl, with her mother's black eyes and hair, and rosy cheeks, and the merry expression which was her inheritance from her father.

Mrs. Barry told Diana she might take Anne out into the garden and show her the flowers. Outside in the garden stood Anne and Diana, gazing bashfully at one another over a clump of gorgeous tiger lilies.

Finally, Anne said, "Oh, Diana, do you think— oh, do you think you can like me a little— enough to be my bosom friend?"

Diana laughed. Diana always laughed before she spoke.

"Why, I guess so," she said. "I'm awfully glad you've come to live at Green Gables. It will be jolly to have someone to play with. There isn't any other girl who lives near enough to play with, and I've no sisters big enough."

When Marilla and Anne went home Diana went with them as far as the log bridge. The two little girls walked with their arms about each other. At the brook they parted with many promises to spend the next afternoon together.

"Well, did you find Diana a kindred spirit?" teased Marilla.

"Oh, yes," sighed Anne. "Oh, Marilla, I'm the happiest girl on Prince Edward Island this very moment."

That night when Anne was in bed and Marilla was in the kitchen with Matthew, Marilla said, "Dear me, it's only three weeks since she came, and it seems as if she'd been here always. I can't imagine the place without her."

A few days later, Anne had truly become bosom friends with Diana. Marilla watched Anne outside telling Matthew of all her adventures, and thought to herself, "I never saw such an infatuated man. The more she talks and the odder the things she says, the more he's delighted evidently." Marilla called Anne in to do her sewing, and immediately Anne began telling Marilla of the upcoming church picnic.

When Marilla said that Anne could go and that she, Marilla, would send along a basket of baked food, Anne exclaimed, "Oh, you dear good Marilla. You are so kind to me. Oh, I'm so much obliged to you."

Then Anne threw herself into Marilla's arms and kissed the woman's cheek. It was the first time in Marilla's whole life that a child had willingly kissed her face. She was secretly vastly pleased at Anne's action, but she said, "There, there, never mind your kissing nonsense."

The special day came at last, and that night a thoroughly happy, completely tired out Anne returned to Green Gables.

"Oh, Marilla, I've had a perfectly scrumptious time. Scrumptious is a new word I learned today. Isn't it very expressive? Everything was lovely. We had a splendid tea and then Mr. Harmon Andrews took us all for a row on the Lake of Shining Waters—six of us at a time. And Jane Andrews nearly fell overboard. She was leaning out to pick water lilies and if Mr. Andrews hadn't caught her by her sash just in the nick of time she'd have fallen in and prob'ly been drowned. I wish it had been me. It would have been such a romantic experience to have been nearly drowned. It would be such a thrilling tale to tell. And we had the ice cream. Words fail me to describe that ice cream. Marilla, I assure you it was sublime."

The way Anne and Diana would go to school was a pretty one. Anne thought those walks to and from school with Diana couldn't be improved upon even by imagination. The Avonlea school was a whitewashed building set back from the road and behind it was a dusky forest and a brook where all the children put their bottles of milk in the morning to keep cool and sweet until the lunch hour.

Marilla had seen Anne start off to school on the first day of September with many secret misgivings. Anne was such an odd girl. How would she get on with the other children? And how on earth would she ever manage to hold her tongue during school hours?

Things went better than Marilla feared, however. Anne came home that first evening in high spirits. "There are a lot of nice girls in school and we had scrumptious fun playing at lunch time. But of course I like Diana best and always will. I'm dreadfully far behind the others. I feel that it's a kind of disgrace. But there's not one of them has such an imagination as I have."

That was three weeks ago and all had gone smoothly so far. But for the first time since school had begun again the girls' favorite, Gilbert Blythe, came to school.

During Latin lessons Diana whispered to Anne, "That's Gilbert Blythe sitting right across the aisle from you. Just look at him and see if you don't think he's handsome."

Anne looked. He was a tall boy, with curly brown hair, hazel eyes, and a teasing smile. He looked back at Anne and winked.

"I think your Gilbert Blythe *is* handsome," whispered Anne to Diana, "but I think he's very bold. It isn't good manners to wink at a strange girl."

That afternoon, Gilbert was trying to make Anne Shirley look at him and failing, because Anne was daydreaming, staring out the window.

Gilbert wasn't used to trying so hard to make a girl look at him and failing. So finally he reached across the aisle, picked up the end of Anne's long red braid, held it out at arm's length and said in a loud whisper, "Carrots! Carrots!"

Anne sprang to her feet. "You mean, hateful boy!" she exclaimed. "How dare you!" And

He reached across the aisle, picked up the end of Anne's long red braid, held it out at arm's length and said in a loud whisper, "Carrots! Carrots!"

then—Thwack! Anne had brought her little chalkboard down on Gilbert's head and cracked it—the chalkboard, not his head—clear across.

Avonlea school always enjoyed a scene. This was an especially enjoyable one. Everybody said, "Oh!" Diana gasped.

Mr. Phillips, the teacher, stalked down the aisle and laid his hand on Anne's shoulder. "Anne Shirley, what does this mean?"

Anne didn't answer. It was too much to expect her to tell before the whole school that she had been called "carrots."

Gilbert spoke up, "It was my fault, Mr. Phillips. I teased her."

Mr. Phillips ignored Gilbert and ordered Anne to stand in front of the blackboard for the rest of the afternoon.

Mr. Phillips wrote on the blackboard above her head: "Anne Shirley has a very bad temper. Anne Shirley must learn to control her temper," and then read it aloud.

Anne decided then and there she would never ever look again at Gilbert Blythe! She would never speak to him!

When school was dismissed Anne marched out with her red head held high. Gilbert tried to stop her at the door. "I'm awful sorry I made fun of your hair, Anne," he whispered. "Honest I am. Don't be mad at me for keeps, now."

Anne went by, without look or sign of hearing.

Anne told Diana on the way home, "I shall

never forgive Gilbert Blythe. He has hurt my feelings *excruciatingly*, Diana."

Anne flung herself into her studies heart and soul, determined not to be outdone in any class by Gilbert. Anne certainly held grudges. She was as intense in her hatreds as in her loves. She would not admit that she meant to rival Gilbert in school work, because that would have been to acknowledge his existence, which Anne ignored; but the rivalry was there and honors went back and forth between them.

Now Gilbert was head of the spelling class; now Anne. One morning Gilbert had all his sums done correctly and had his name written on the blackboard on the roll of honor; the next morning Anne, having worked hard on decimals the entire evening before, would be first. One awful day they were ties and their names were written up together. When the written tests at the end of each month were held the suspense was terrible. The first month Gilbert came out three marks ahead. The second Anne beat him by five. By the end of the term Anne and Gilbert were both promoted into the fifth class.

Part IV

Adventure and Romance

SUMMER CAME once more to Green Gables, after a beautiful, capricious, reluctant Canadian spring, and no one looked forward to the two months' vacation more than Anne. One of the social highlights of the season was Diana's tea party. "Small and select," Anne assured Marilla. "Just the girls in our class." They had a good time and nothing bad happened until after tea, when they found themselves in the garden. "Daring" was the fashionable amusement among the Avonlea children just then. It had begun among the boys, but soon spread to the girls, and all the silly things that were done in Avonlea that summer because children were "dared" to do them would fill a book.

The girls played a round of dares which included Anne daring Josie Pye to walk along the top of the garden's board-fence. Josie Pye successfully accomplished this dare and then had her turn with Anne.

"I dare you to climb up there and walk the ridge of Mr. Barry's kitchen roof," said Josie.

"Don't you do it!" said Diana. "You'll fall off

and be killed. It isn't fair to dare anybody to do anything so dangerous."

"I must do it. My honor is at stake," said Anne. "I shall walk that roofline, Diana, or perish in the attempt."

Anne climbed the ladder amid the girls' breathless silence, got to the roof, balanced herself on that dangerous edge, and started to walk along it, dizzy and realizing that walking rooflines was not something for which your imagination helped you out much. She managed to take several steps before she swayed, lost her balance, stumbled, staggered, and fell, sliding down over the sun-baked roof and crashing off it through the vines beneath—all before the frightened girls below could even shriek.

"Anne, are you killed?" cried Diana, throwing herself on her knees beside her friend. "Oh, Anne, dear Anne, speak just one word to me and tell me if you're killed."

"No, Diana," said Anne, sitting up, "I am not killed."

Mrs. Barry came running out of the house. Anne tried to get up but sank back again with a sharp cry of pain.

"What's the matter? Where have you hurt yourself?" demanded Mrs. Barry.

"My ankle," said Anne.

Marilla was out in the orchard picking apples when she saw Mr. Barry coming over the log bridge and up the slope, with Mrs. Barry beside him and a whole parade of girls trailing after him. In his arms he carried Anne, whose head lay againt his shoulder.

At that moment, Marilla realized what Anne had come to mean to her. She would have admitted that she liked Anne—even that she was very fond of Anne. But now she knew as she hurried down the slope that Anne was dearer to her than anything on earth.

"Don't be very frightened, Marilla," said Anne. "I was walking the roofline and I fell off. I expect I have sprained my ankle. But, Marilla, I might have broken my neck. Let us look on the bright side of things."

Matthew, called to come from a distant field, was sent off for the doctor, who discovered that Anne's ankle was broken.

That night, when Marilla went up to Anne's room, Anne's pained voice said, "Aren't you very sorry for me, Marilla?"

"It was your own fault," said Marilla.

"And that is just why you should be sorry for me," said Anne, "because the thought that it is all my own fault is what makes it so hard. If I could blame it on anybody I would feel so much better. But what would you have done, Marilla, if you had been dared to walk a roofline?"

"I'd have stayed on good firm ground and let them dare away. Such absurdity!"

"But you have such strength of mind, Marilla. I haven't," said Anne. "And I think I have been punished so much that you needn't be very cross with me, Marilla. I won't be able to go around for six or seven weeks and I'll miss the new lady teacher. And Gil—everybody will get ahead of me in class. But I'll try to bear it all bravely if only you won't be cross with me, Marilla."

"There, there, I'm not cross," said Marilla.

It was October again when Anne was ready to go back to school—a glorious October, all red and gold. In the new teacher, Miss Stacy, Anne found another true and helpful friend, and she expanded like a flower under this wholesome influence.

In November Miss Stacy announced a project for a Christmas concert by the Avonlea students. "We're going to have six choruses and Diana is up to sing a solo," Anne told Marilla. "I'm in two dialogues, and I'm to have two recitations. I just tremble when I think of it, but it's a nice thrilly kind of tremble. I know you are not so excited as I am, Marilla, but don't you hope your little Anne will do well?"

"All I hope is that you'll behave yourself. I'll be heartily glad when all this fuss is over and you'll be able to settle down. You are simply good for nothing just now with your head stuffed full of dialogues. As for your tongue, it's a marvel it's not clean worn out."

Anne sighed and went outside, where Matthew was chopping wood. Anne perched herself on a block and talked the concert over with him.

"Well now," he said, "I reckon it's going to be a pretty good concert. And I expect you'll do your part fine." Matthew smiled. Anne smiled back at him. Those two were the best of friends.

One cold gray evening that December Matthew came into the kitchen and sat down in the woodbox corner to take off his heavy boots. All of a sudden Anne and a number of her schoolmates, who had been practicing a little play for the concert, came trooping through the hall and into the kitchen, laughing and chatting. Matthew shrank back into shadows of the corner, unnoticed by them, and watched them for ten minutes as they put on their caps and jackets and talked about the little play and the concert. Anne stood among them, as bright-eyed and lively as they; but Matthew suddenly saw that there was something about her different from her friends. Anne was not dressed like the other girls!

The more Matthew thought about the matter later that evening the more he was convinced that Anne never had been dressed like the other girls—never since she had come to Green Gables. Marilla kept her clothed in plain, dark dresses, all made after the same pattern. Marilla knew best and Marilla was bringing her up. But surely it would do no harm to let the child have one pretty dress—something like Diana Barry always wore. Matthew decided that he would give her one. Christmas was only two weeks away. A nice new dress would be the very thing for a present.

The very next evening Matthew went to Mrs. Lynde to ask for advice.

"Pick out a dress for you to give Anne?" said Rachel. "To be sure I will. I'm going to town tomorrow and I'll attend to it. Have you something in particular in mind? No? Well, I'll just go by my own judgment then. Perhaps you'd like me to make it up for her, too, seeing that if Marilla was to make it Anne would probably get wind of it before the time and spoil the surprise? Well, I'll do it. No, it isn't a mite of trouble. I like sewing."

"Well now, I'm much obliged," said Matthew, "and—and—I dunno—but I'd like—I think they make the sleeves different nowadays to what they used to be. If it wouldn't be asking too much I—I'd like them to be made in the new way."

"Puffs? Of course. You needn't worry a speck more about it, Matthew. I'll make it up in the very latest fashion," said Mrs. Lynde.

Marilla knew all the following two weeks that Matthew had something on his mind, but what it was she could not guess, until Christmas Eve, when Mrs. Lynde brought up the new dress.

"So this is what Matthew has been looking so mysterious over and grinning about to himself for two weeks, is it?" she said. "I knew he was up to some foolishness. Well, I must say I don't think Anne needed any more dresses. I made her three good, serviceable ones this fall, and anything more is sheer extravagance. You'll pamper Anne's vanity, Matthew, and she's as vain as a peacock now."

Christmas morning broke on a beautiful white world. Anne ran downstairs singing.

"Merry Christmas, Marilla! Merry Christmas, Matthew! Isn't it a lovely Christmas? I'm so glad it's white. —Why—why, Matthew, is that for me? Oh, Matthew!"

Matthew had unfolded the dress from its paper and held it out. Anne took the dress and looked at it in silence. Oh, how pretty it was—a lovely soft brown with all the gloss of silk; a skirt with dainty frills. But the sleeves—they were the crowning glory! Long elbow cuffs, and above them two beautiful puffs.

"That's a Christmas present for you, Anne," said Matthew. "Why—why—Anne, don't you like it? Well now—well now."

For Anne's eyes had suddenly filled with tears.

"Like it! Oh, Matthew! It's perfectly exquisite. Oh, I can never thank you enough. Look at those sleeves! Oh, it seems to me this must be a happy dream."

"Well, well, let us have breakfast," interrupted Marilla. "I must say, Anne, I don't think you needed the dress; but since Matthew has got it for you, see that you take good care of it. There's

Oh, how pretty it was—a lovely soft brown with all the gloss of silk; a skirt with dainty frills. But the sleeves—they were the crowning glory!

a hair ribbon Mrs. Lynde left for you. It's brown, to match the dress. Come now, sit down."

"I don't see how I'm going to eat breakfast," said Anne. "Breakfast seems so commonplace at such an exciting moment. I'd rather feast my eyes on that dress."

That day all the Avonlea students were in a fever of excitement decorating the hall for the Christmas concert, which was a huge success. Later that night Marilla and Matthew, who had been out to a concert for the first time in twenty years, sat for a while by the kitchen fire after Anne had gone to bed.

"Well now, I guess our Anne did as well as any of them," said Matthew proudly.

"Yes, she did," admitted Marilla. "She's a bright child, Matthew. And she looked real nice, too, in her new dress. I've been kind of opposed to this concert scheme, but I suppose there's no real harm in it after all. Anyhow, I was proud of Anne tonight, although I'm not going to tell her so."

"Well now, I was proud of her and I did tell her so before she went upstairs," said Matthew.

The winter weeks slipped by. It was an unusually mild winter, with so little snow that Anne and Diana could go to school nearly every day by way of the Birch Path. On Anne's birthday they were tripping lightly down it, when Anne said, "Just think, Diana, I'm thirteen years old today. I can scarcely realize that I'm in my teens. It makes life seem much more interesting."

One evening in early spring Marilla came home and discovered that Anne was nowhere to be seen. Marilla was sure Anne was off gadding about with Diana. Dinner came and went, and there was still no Anne. After dinner Marilla went upstairs and into Anne's room where she discovered Anne herself lying on the bed, face down on the pillows.

"Mercy on us," said Marilla, "have you been asleep, Anne?"

"No," was the muffled answer.

"Are you sick then?" demanded Marilla, going over to the bed.

"No. But please, Marilla, go away and don't look at me. I'm in the depths of despair and I don't care who gets ahead in class or writes the best composition or sings in the Sunday-school choir any more. My career is closed. Marilla, go away and don't look at me."

"Anne Shirley, whatever is the matter with you? What have you done? Get right up this minute and tell me."

Anne slid to the floor. "Look at my hair," she whispered.

"Anne Shirley! What have you done to your hair? Why, it's *green!*" Never in her life had Marilla seen anything so grotesque as Anne's hair.

"Yes, it's green," said Anne. "I thought nothing

could be as bad as red hair. But now I know it's ten times worse to have green hair. Oh, Marilla, you little know how utterly wretched I am."

"Tell me just what you've done. I've been expecting something silly for some time. Now, then, what did you do to your hair?"

"I dyed it."

"Dyed it! If I'd decided it was worth while to dye my hair I'd have dyed it a decent color at least. I wouldn't have dyed it green."

"But I didn't mean to dye it green, Marilla. The peddler who was here this afternoon said it would turn my hair a beautiful raven black. How could I doubt his word, Marilla?"

"Anne Shirley, how often have I told you never to let one of those peddlers in the house!"

"Oh, I didn't let him in the house. I went out, carefully shut the door, and looked at his things on the step. He had a big box of very interesting things. I saw the bottle of hair dye. The peddler said it was guaranteed to dye any hair a beautiful raven black and wouldn't wash off. The temptation was irresistible. So I bought it, and as soon as he had gone I came up here and applied it with an old hairbrush as the directions said. I used up the whole bottle."

Anne washed her hair that night, scrubbing it with soap and water, but indeed the dye wouldn't wash off.

"Oh, Marilla, what shall I do?" asked Anne in tears. "I can never live this down. People have pretty well forgotten my other mistakes, but they'll never forget this."

Anne's unhappiness continued for a week. During that time she went nowhere and shampooed her hair every day. At the end of the week Marilla said, "It's no use, Anne. That dye is set. Your hair must be cut off; there is no other way. You can't go out looking like that."

Anne's clipped head made a sensation in school the following Monday, but to her relief nobody guessed the real reason for it.

The next summer was one of adventure for Anne and her friends. Now that they were big girls of thirteen they were too old for many of their childish amusements. But this summer there was the pond below Diana's house, where they fished for trout and learned to row in Mr. Barry's little flat-bottomed boat.

One day Anne had the marvelous idea to dramatize Elaine, the fair lily maid from Tennyson's poem, which they had studied in school the preceding winter. Anne's plan was hailed with enthusiasm. The girls had discovered that if the flat were pushed off from the landing place it would drift down with the current under the bridge and finally strand itself on another headland lower down the brook. They had often gone down like this and nothing could be more convenient for playing Elaine.

"Well, I'll be Elaine," said Anne, finally yielding

to her friends' insistence that she play the forlorn maid—even though her hair *was* red. "Ruby, you must be King Arthur and Jane will be Guinevere and Diana must be Lancelot. We must pall the barge all its length in blackest samite. That old black shawl of your mother's will be just the thing, Diana."

The black shawl having been procured, Anne spread it over the flat and then lay down on the bottom, with closed eyes and hands folded over her breast. "Oh, she does look really dead," whispered Ruby nervously, watching the still, white little face under the flickering shadows of the birches. "It makes me feel frightened."

Since a white lily was not obtainable just then, a tall blue iris placed in one of Anne's folded hands was all that could be desired.

"Now she's all ready," said Jane. "We must kiss her quiet brows and, Diana, you say, 'Sister, farewell for ever.' Anne, for goodness sake smile a little. You know Elaine 'lay as though she smiled.' Now push the flat off."

The flat was accordingly pushed off, and the other girls scampered up through the woods and down to the lower headland. For a few minutes Anne, drifting slowly down, enjoyed the romance of her situation to the full. Then something happened not at all romantic. The flat began to leak. In a very few moments it was necessary for Elaine to scramble to her feet and gaze blankly at a big crack in the bottom of her barge through which the water was literally pouring. At this rate, the flat would fill and sink long before it could drift to the lower headland.

Anne gave one gasping little scream which nobody heard; she was white to the lips, but she did not lose her self-possession. There was one chance—just one.

"I was horribly frightened," she told Miss Stacy the next day, "and it seemed like years while the flat was drifting and the water rising in it every moment. I prayed most earnestly, for I knew the only way God could save me was to let the flat drift close enough to one of the bridge piles for me to climb up on it. My prayer was answered, for the flat bumped right into a pile for a minute and I scrambled up. And there I was, clinging to that slippery old pile with no way of getting up or down. It was a very unromantic position."

The flat drifted under the bridge and then promptly sank in midstream, as Anne watched, clinging desperately to her precarious foothold. The minutes passed by, each seeming an hour to the unfortunate lily maid. Then, just as she thought she really could not endure the ache in her arms and wrists another moment, Gilbert Blythe came rowing under the bridge!

"Anne Shirley! How on earth did you get there?" he exclaimed. Without waiting for an answer he pulled up close to the pile and extended his hand. There was no help for it; Anne, clinging to Gilbert's hand, scrambled down into the boat, where she sat, furious, in the stern with her arms full of dripping shawl.

Gilbert obligingly rowed to the landing and Anne, disdaining assistance, sprang nimbly on shore.

"I'm very much obliged to you," she said haughtily as she turned away. "Anne," said Gilbert hurriedly, "can't we be friends? I'm awfully sorry I made fun of your hair that time. I only meant it for a joke. Let's be friends."

For a moment Anne hesitated. But the bitterness of her old grievance promptly stiffened up her wavering determination.

"No," she said coldly, "I shall never be friends with you, Gilbert Blythe!"

"All right!" Gilbert replied angrily, springing into his skiff. "I'll never ask you to be friends again, Anne Shirley. And I don't care either!"

He pulled away with swift, defiant strokes, and Anne went up the steep path. She held her head very high, but she was conscious of an odd feeling of regret. She almost wished she had answered Gilbert differently.

Great was the consternation in the Barry and Cuthbert households when the events of the afternoon became known.

"Will you *ever* have any sense, Anne?" groaned Marilla.

"Oh, yes, I think I will, Marilla," returned Anne optimistically. "I think my prospects of becoming sensible are brighter now than ever. I have come to the conclusion that it is no use trying to be romantic in Avonlea. It was probably easy enough in towered Camelot hundreds of years ago, but romance is not appreciated now. I feel quite sure that you will soon see a great improvement in me in this respect, Marilla."

Part V
Anne Makes the Grade

O NE LATE AFTERNOON in November when Anne fell asleep in the kitchen, Marilla looked at her with tenderness. She had learned to love this slim, gray-eyed girl with a deep and strong affection. She had a feeling that it was rather sinful to love anyone so intensely, and so she hid her feelings and even made herself stricter and more critical than she would have been if the girl had been less dear to her. Certainly Anne herself had no idea how Marilla loved her.

While Anne had been off playing with Diana earlier that afternoon, Miss Stacy had come to talk about Anne to Marilla and Matthew; she asked if they would agree to Anne getting extra lessons after school so that she could study for the entrance exam at Queen's Academy and become a teacher. Marilla told Anne they had agreed to pay for her lessons. The exam was not for a year and a half, but Anne promised that she would study hard and do her best to pass.

"Oh, Marilla, thank you," Anne had said, flinging her arms around Marilla. "I'm extremely grateful to you and Matthew. I shall take more interest than ever in my studies."

There was open rivalry between Gilbert and Anne now. Before the rivalry had been rather one-sided, but there was no longer any doubt that Gilbert was as determined to be first in class as Anne was.

Since Anne had ignored Gilbert and not forgiven him for so long, he now ignored Anne. She found that it is not pleasant to be ignored. She told herself that she did not care, but deep down she knew that she did, and wished that she had forgiven him. She found that she no longer hated him for having said "Carrots!" at her so long ago.

The winter passed away in a round of pleasant duties and studies. Anne was happy, eager, interested; there were lessons to be learned and honors to be won; delightful books to read; pleasant Saturday afternoons with Diana; and then, almost before Anne realized it, spring had come again to Green Gables and all the world was abloom once more. Teacher and students were alike glad when the term ended and the glad vacation days stretched before them.

Anne had the golden summer of her life as far as freedom and frolic went. She walked, rowed, picked berries and dreamed to her heart's content; and when September came she was bright-eyed and alert.

"I feel just like studying with all my might,"

she declared as she brought her books down from the attic. "Oh, you good old friends, I'm glad to see your honest faces once more—yes, even you, geometry."

Miss Stacy came back to Avonlea school and found all her pupils eager for work once more. Especially did the students for the Queen's exam gear up, because that exam loomed for them at the end of the coming year. Suppose they did not pass! That thought haunted Anne all winter. When she had bad dreams she saw herself staring at the pass lists of the exam, where Gilbert Blythe's name was at the top and where hers did not appear at all.

Meanwhile Anne grew, shooting up so rapidly that Marilla was astonished one day, when they were standing side by side, to find the girl was taller than herself.

"Why, Anne, how you've grown!" she sighed. Marilla was almost sorry. The child she had learned to love had vanished somehow and here was this tall, serious-eyed girl of fifteen, with the thoughtful brow and the proud little head, in her place. Marilla loved the girl as much as she had loved the child, but she was aware of a strange sense of loss. And that night, when Anne had gone to prayer meeting with Diana, Marilla sat alone in the wintry twilight and let herself cry. Matthew, coming in with a lantern, caught her at it and gazed at her in such confusion that Marilla had to laugh through her tears.

"I was thinking about Anne," she explained. "She's got to be such a big girl—and she'll probably be away from us next winter. I'll miss her terrible."

"She'll be able to come home often," said Matthew. "The railroad will be built near town by then."

"It won't be the same as having her here all the time," said Marilla.

There were other changes in Anne no less real than the physical change. For one thing, she became much quieter. Marilla pointed this out to her.

"You don't chatter half as much as you used to, Anne, nor use half as many big words. What has come over you?"

Anne blushed and laughed a little, as she dropped her book and looked out of the window, where springtime was beginning.

"I don't know—I don't want to talk as much. It's nicer to think dear, pretty thoughts and keep them in one's heart, like treasures. I don't like to have them laughed at or wondered over. It's fun to be almost grown up in some ways, but it's not the kind of fun I expected, Marilla. There's so much to learn and do and think that there isn't time for big words."

"You've only got two months before the entrance examination," said Marilla. "Do you think you'll be able to get through?"

"I don't know. Sometimes I think I'll be all

right—and then I get horribly afraid. It haunts me. Sometimes I wake up in the night and wonder what I'll do if I don't pass."

"Why, go to school next year and try again," said Marilla.

"Oh, I don't believe I'd have the heart for it. It would be such a disgrace to fail, especially if Gil—if the others passed."

In June the Queen's entrance students went to the city for the exam. Anne had promised Diana that she would write, and she was faithful to her word.

"Dearest Diana," wrote Anne, "here it is Tuesday night and I'm writing to you as promised. Last night I was horribly lonesome all alone in my room and wished so much you were with me. I couldn't 'cram' because I'd promised Miss Stacy not to, but it was as hard to keep from opening my history as it used to be to keep me from reading a story before my lessons were learned.

"This morning Miss Stacy came for me and we went to the Academy, calling for Jane and Ruby and Josie on our way. Ruby asked me to feel her hands and they were cold as ice. Josie said I looked as if I hadn't slept a wink and she didn't believe I was strong enough to stand the grind of the teacher's course even if I did get through. There are times and seasons even yet when I don't feel that I've made any great headway in learning to like Josie Pye!

"When we reached the Academy there were scores of students there from all over the Island. The first person we saw was Moody Spurgeon sitting on the steps and muttering away to himself. Jane asked him what on earth he was doing and he said he was repeating the multiplication table over and over to steady his nerves and for pity's sake not to interrupt him, because if he stopped for a moment he got frightened and forgot everything he ever knew, but the multiplication table kept all his facts firmly in their proper place!

"When we were assigned to our rooms Miss Stacy had to leave us. Jane and I sat together and Jane was so composed that I envied her. No need of the multiplication table for good, steady, sensible Jane! I wondered if I looked as I felt and if they could hear my heart thumping clear across the room. Then a man came in and began distributing the English examination sheets. My hands grew cold then and my head fairly whirled round as I picked it up. Just one awful moment,—Diana, I felt exactly as I did four years ago when I asked Marilla if I might stay at Green Gables—and then everything cleared up in my mind and my heart began beating again—I forgot to say that it had stopped altogether!—for I knew I could do something with *that* paper anyhow.

"At noon we went home for dinner and then back again for history in the afternoon. The history was a pretty hard paper and I got dreadfully mixed up in the dates. Still, I think I did fairly well today. But oh, Diana, tomorrow the geometry exam comes off and when I think of it it takes every bit of determination I possess to keep from opening my Euclid. If I thought the multiplication table would help me any I would recite it from now till tomorrow morning.

"I went down to see the other girls this evening. On my way I met Moody Spurgeon wandering distractedly around. He said he knew he had failed in history and he was born to be a disappointment to his parents and he was going home on the morning train; and it would be easier to be a carpenter than a minister, anyhow. I cheered him up and persuaded him to stay to the end because it would be unfair to Miss Stacy if he didn't. Sometimes I have wished I was born a boy, but when I see Moody Spurgeon I'm always glad I'm a girl and not his sister.

"Ruby was in hysterics when I reached their boarding-house; she had just discovered a fearful mistake she had made in her English paper. When she recovered we went up-town and had an ice-cream. How we wished you had been with us.

"Oh, Diana, if only the geometry examination were over! But there, as Mrs. Lynde would say, the sun will go on rising and setting whether I fail in geometry or not. That is true but not especially comforting. I think I'd rather it *didn't* go on if I failed!

"Yours devotedly.
"ANNE."

The geometry examination and all the others were over in due time and Anne arrived home on Friday evening, rather tired but with an air of chastened triumph about her. Diana was over at Green Gables when she arrived and they met as if they had been parted for years.

"You old darling, it's perfectly splendid to see you back again. It seems like an age since you went to town and oh, Anne, how did you get along?"

"Pretty well, I think, in everything but the

geometry. I don't know whether I passed in it or not and I have a creepy, crawly presentiment that I didn't. Oh, how good it is to be back! Green Gables is the dearest, loveliest spot in the world."

"How did the others do?"

"The girls say they know they didn't pass, but I think they did pretty well. Josie says the geometry was so easy a child of ten could do it! Moody Spurgeon still thinks he failed in history and Charlie says he failed in algebra. But we don't really know anything about it and won't until the pass list is out. That won't be for a fortnight. Fancy living a fortnight in such suspense! I wish I could go to sleep and never wake up until it is over."

Diana knew it would be useless to ask how Gilbert Blythe had fared, so she merely said:

"Oh, you'll pass all right. Don't worry."

"I'd rather not pass at all than not come out pretty well up on the list," flashed Anne, by which she meant—and Diana knew she meant—that success would be incomplete and bitter if she did not come out ahead of Gilbert Blythe.

With this end in view Anne had strained every nerve during the examinations. So had Gilbert. But Anne had another and better motive for wishing to do well. She wanted to "pass high" for the sake of Matthew and Marilla—especially Matthew. Matthew had declared to her his conviction that she "would beat the whole Island."

After two weeks Anne and the other students began to wait around the post office to get the newspapers that would announce their successes or failures. But when three weeks had gone by without the pass list appearing Anne began to feel that she really couldn't stand the strain much longer.

Then, one evening, the news came. Diana came rushing to Green Gables with a newspaper.

"Anne, you've passed," she cried, "passed the very first—you and Gilbert both—you're ties—but your name is first. Oh, I'm so proud! Oh, Anne, what does it feel like to see your name at the head of a pass list like that? You're as calm and cool as a spring evening."

"I'm just dazzled inside," said Anne. "I want to say a hundred things, and I can't find the words to say them in. Excuse me a minute, Diana. I must run right out to the field to tell Matthew."

They hurried to the hayfield where Matthew was, and, as luck would have it, Mrs. Lynde was talking to Marilla there.

"Oh, Matthew," exclaimed Anne, "I've passed and I'm first—or one of the first! I'm not vain, but I'm thankful."

"Well now, I always said it," said Matthew, gazing at the newspaper and Anne's name. "I knew you could beat them all easy."

"You've done pretty well, I must say, Anne," said Marilla.

Mrs. Lynde spoke up as well, "You're a credit to your friends, Anne, and we're all proud of you."

August was very busy at Green Gables, for

Anne was getting ready to go to Queen's Academy, and there was much sewing to be done, and many things to be talked over and arranged.

Marilla even made Anne an evening dress.

"Oh, Marilla, it's just lovely," said Anne. "Thank you so much. I don't believe you ought to be so kind to me—it's making it harder every day for me to go away."

Anne put on the dress one evening for Matthew's and Marilla's benefit and recited a poem for them in the kitchen.

As Marilla watched the bright, lively face and graceful motions of Anne, her thoughts went back to the evening Anne had arrived at Green Gables, and memory recalled a vivid picture of the odd, frightened child in her old, ugly dress. Something in the memory brought tears to Marilla's eyes.

"I declare, my performance has made you cry, Marilla," said Anne, stooping over Marilla's chair to drop a quick kiss on that lady's cheek.

"No, I wasn't crying over your piece," said Marilla. "I just couldn't help thinking of the little girl you used to be, Anne. And I was wishing you could have stayed a little girl, even with all your odd ways. You've grown up now and you're going away; and you look so stylish and so—so—different in that dress—as if you didn't belong in Avonlea at all—and I just got lonesome thinking it over."

"Marilla!" Anne sat down on Marilla's lap, took Marilla's lined face between her hands, and looked gravely and tenderly into Marilla's eyes. "I'm not a bit changed—not really. I'm only just pruned down and branched out. The real me—back here—is just the same. At heart I shall always be your little Anne, who will love you and Matthew and dear Green Gables more and better every day of her life."

Marilla could not speak her feelings but put her arms close about the girl and held her tenderly to her heart, wishing that she need never let her go.

Matthew, his eyes moist, got up and went out-of-doors. To himself he muttered, "She's been a blessing to us, and there never was a luckier mistake than what Mrs. Spencer made—if it *was* luck. I don't believe it was any such thing. It was Fate, because the Almighty saw we needed her, I reckon."

The day finally came when Anne must go to town. She and Matthew drove in one fine September morning after a tearful parting with Diana and an untearful parting with Marilla. But that night, when Marilla went to bed, aware that the little room at the end of the hall was empty of Anne, she buried her face in her pillow and wept, sobbing for her girl.

Anne and the rest of the Avonlea scholars reached town just in time to hurry off to the Academy. That first day passed pleasantly enough in a whirl of excitement, meeting all the new students, learning to know the professors by sight and being assorted and organized into classes. Anne intended taking up the second year work, being advised to do so by Miss Stacy; Gilbert Blythe elected to do the same. This meant getting a First Class teacher's license in one year instead of two, if they were successful; but it also meant much more and harder work. Jane, Ruby, Josie, Charlie, and Moody Spurgeon, not being troubled with the stirrings of ambition, were content to take up the first year work. Anne was conscious of a pang of loneliness when she found herself in a room with fifty other students, not one of whom she knew, except the tall, brown-haired boy across the room; and knowing him in the fashion she did, did not help her much, as she reflected pessimistically. Yet she was undeniably glad that they were in the same class; the old rivalry could still be carried on, and Anne would hardly have known what to do if it had been lacking.

"I wouldn't feel comfortable without it," she thought. "Gilbert looks awfully determined. I suppose he's making up his mind, here and now, to win the medal. What a splendid chin he has! I never noticed it before. I do wish Jane and Ruby had gone in for First Class, too. I suppose I won't feel so much like a cat in a strange garret when I get acquainted, though. I wonder which of the girls here are going to be my friends. It's really an interesting speculation. Of course I promised Diana that no Queen's girl, no matter how much I liked her, should ever be as dear to me as she is; but I've lots of second-best affections to bestow. I like the look of that girl with the brown eyes and crimson waist. She looks vivid and red-rosy; there's that pale, fair one gazing out of the window. She has lovely hair, and looks as if she knew a thing or two about dreams. I'd like to know them both—know them well—well enough to walk with my arm about their waists, and call them nicknames. But just now I don't know them and they don't know me, and probably don't want to know me particularly. Oh, it's lonesome!"

It was lonesomer still when Anne found herself alone in her hall bedroom that night at twilight. She was not to board with the other girls, who all had relatives in town to take pity on them. She looked dismally about her narrow little room, with its dull-papered, pictureless walls, its small iron bedstead and empty bookcase; and a horrible choke came into her throat as she thought of her own white room at Green Gables, where she would have the pleasant consciousness of a great green still outdoors, of sweet peas growing in the garden, and moonlight falling on the orchard, of the brook below the slope and the spruce boughs tossing in the night wind beyond it, of a vast starry sky, and the light from Diana's window shining out through the gap in the trees. Here there was nothing of this;

Anne knew that outside of her window was a hard street, with a network of telephone wires shutting out the sky, the tramp of alien feet, and a thousand lights gleaming on stranger faces. She knew that she was going to cry, and fought against it.

"I *won't* cry. It's silly—and weak—there's the third tear splashing down by my nose. There are more coming! I must think of something funny to stop them. But there's nothing funny except what is connected with Avonlea, and that only makes things worse—four—five—I'm going home next Friday, but that seems a hundred years away. Oh, Matthew is nearly home by now—and Marilla is at the gate, looking down the lane for him— six—seven—eight—oh, there's no use in counting them! They're coming in a flood presently. I can't cheer up—I don't *want* to cheer up. It's nicer to be miserable!"

Anne worked hard, though missing Matthew and Marilla at Green Gables. When the possibility of a scholarship to Redmond College came up, Anne was determined to win it. "Wouldn't Matthew be proud if I got a B.A.?"

Anne's homesickness wore off, greatly helped in the wearing by her weekend visits to Green Gables. As long as the open weather lasted the Avonlea students went home on the new branch railway every Friday night. Diana and several other Avonlea young folks were generally on hand to meet them and they all walked over to Avonlea in a merry party. Anne thought those Friday evening gypsyings over the autumnal hills in the crisp golden air, with the homelights of Avonlea twinkling beyond, were the best and dearest hours in the whole week.

Gilbert Blythe nearly always walked with Ruby Gillis and carried her satchel for her. Ruby was a very handsome young lady; she wore her skirts as long as her mother would let her and did her hair up in town, though she had to take it down when she went home. She had large, bright-blue eyes, a brilliant complexion, and a plump showy figure. She laughed a great deal, was cheerful and good-tempered, and enjoyed the pleasant things of life frankly.

"But I shouldn't think she was the sort of girl Gilbert would like," whispered Jane to Anne. Anne did not think so either, but she would not have said so for the Avery scholarship. She could not help thinking, too, that it would be very pleasant to have such a friend as Gilbert to jest and chatter with and exchange ideas about books and studies and ambitions. Gilbert had ambitions, she knew, and Ruby Gillis did not seem the sort of person with whom such could be profitably discussed.

There was no silly sentiment in Anne's ideas concerning Gilbert. Boys were to her, when she thought about them at all, merely possible good comrades. If she and Gilbert had been friends she would not have cared how many other friends he had nor with whom he walked. She had a genius for friendship; girl friends she had in plenty; but she had a vague consciousness that masculine friendship might also be a good thing to round out one's conceptions of companionship and furnish broader standpoints of judgment and comparison. Not that Anne could have put her feelings on the matter into just such clear definition. But she thought that if Gilbert had ever walked home with her from the train, over the crisp fields and along the ferny byways, they might have had many and merry and interesting conversations about the new world that was opening around them and their hopes and ambitions therein. Gilbert was a clever young fellow, with his own thoughts about things and a determination to get the best out of life and put the best into it. Ruby Gillis told Jane Andrews that she didn't understand half the things Gilbert Blythe said; he talked just like Anne Shirley did when she had a thoughtful fit on and for her part she didn't think it any fun to be bothering about books and that sort of thing when you didn't have to.

After Christmas Anne worked even harder and more steadily. Her rivalry with Gilbert was as intense as it had ever been in Avonlea school, but somehow the bitterness had gone out of it.

Then, almost before anybody realized it, spring had come; out in Avonlea the Mayflowers were peeping pinkly out on the sere barrens where snow-wreaths lingered; and the "mist of green" was on the woods and in the valleys. But in Charlottetown harassed Queen's students thought and talked only of examinations.

"It doesn't seem possible that the term is nearly over," said Anne. "Why, last fall it seemed so long to look forward to—a whole winter of studies and classes. And here we are, with the exams looming up next week. Girls, sometimes I feel as if those exams meant everything, but when I look at the big buds swelling on those chestnut trees and the misty blue air at the end of the streets they don't seem half so important."

Jane and Ruby and Josie, who had dropped in, did not take this view of it. To them the coming examinations were very important indeed—far more important than chestnut buds or Maytime hazes. It was all very well for Anne, who was sure of passing at least, to have her moments of belittling them, but when your whole future depended on them—as the girls truly thought theirs did—you could not regard them philosophically.

"I've lost seven pounds in the last two weeks," sighed Jane. "It's no use to say don't worry. I *will* worry. Worrying helps you some—it seems as if you were doing something when you're worrying. It would be dreadful if I failed to get my license after going to Queen's all winter and spending so much money."

"*I* don't care," said Josie Pye. "If I don't pass

this year I'm coming back next. My father can afford to send me. Anne, Frank Stockley says that Professor Tremaine said Gilbert Blythe was sure to get the medal and that Emily Clay would likely win the Avery scholarship."

"That may make me feel badly tomorrow, Josie," laughed Anne, "but just now I honestly feel that as long as I know the violets are coming out all purple down in the hollow below Green Gables and that little ferns are poking their heads up in Lovers' Lane, it's not a great deal of difference whether I win the Avery or not. I've done my best and I begin to understand what is meant by the 'joy of the strife.' Next to trying and winning, the best thing is trying and failing. Girls, don't talk about exams! Look at that arch of pale green sky over those houses and picture to yourselves what it must look like over the purply-dark beechwoods back of Avonlea."

"What are you going to wear for commencement, Jane?" asked Ruby practically.

Jane and Josie both answered at once and the chatter drifted into a side eddy of fashions. But Anne, with her elbows on the window sill, her soft cheek laid against her clasped hands, and her eyes filled with visions, looked out unheedingly across city roof and spire to that glorious dome of sunset sky and wove her dreams of a possible future from the golden tissue of youth's own optimism. All the Beyond was hers with its possibilities lurking rosily in the oncoming years—each year a rose of promise to be woven into an immortal chaplet.

On the morning when the final results of all the examinations were to be posted on the bulletin board at Queen's, Anne and Jane walked down the street together. Jane was smiling and happy; examinations were over and she was comfortably sure she had made a pass at least; further considerations troubled Jane not at all; she had no soaring ambitions and consequently was not affected with the unrest attendant thereon. Anne was pale and quiet; in ten more minutes she would know who had won the medal and who the Avery. Beyond those ten minutes there did not seem, just then, to be anything worth being called Time.

"Of course you'll win one of them anyhow," said Jane, who couldn't understand how the faculty could be so unfair as to order it otherwise.

"I have no hope of the Avery," said Anne. "Everybody says Emily Clay will win it. And I'm not going to march up to that bulletin board and look at it before everybody. I haven't the moral courage. I'm going straight to the girls' dressing room. You must read the announcements and then come and tell me, Jane. And I implore you in the name of our old friendship to do it as quickly as possible. If I have failed just say so, without trying to break it gently; and whatever you do *don't* sympathize with me. Promise me this, Jane."

Jane promised solemnly; but, as it happened, there was no necessity for such a promise. When they went up the entrance steps of Queen's they found the hall full of boys who were carrying Gilbert Blythe around on their shoulders and yelling at the tops of their voices, "Hurrah for Blythe, Medalist!"

For a moment Anne felt one sickening pang of defeat and disappointment. So she had failed and Gilbert had won! Well, Matthew would be sorry—he had been so sure she would win.

And then!

Somebody called out:

"Three cheers for Miss Shirley, winner of the Avery!"

"Oh, Anne," gasped Jane, as they fled to the girls' dressing room amid hearty cheers. "Oh, Anne, I'm so proud! Isn't it splendid?"

And then the girls were around them and Anne was the center of a laughing, congratulating group. Her shoulders were thumped and her hands shaken vigorously. She was pushed and pulled and hugged and among it all she managed to whisper to Jane:

"Oh, won't Matthew and Marilla be pleased! I must write the news home right away."

Commencement was the next important happening. The exercises were held in the big assembly hall of the Academy. Addresses were given, essays read, songs sung, the public award of diplomas, prizes and medals made.

Matthew and Marilla were there, with eyes and ears for only one student on the platform—a tall girl in pale green, with faintly flushed cheeks and starry eyes, who read the best essay and was pointed out and whispered about as the Avery winner.

"Reckon you're glad we kept her, Marilla?" whispered Matthew, speaking for the first time since he had entered the hall, when Anne had finished her essay.

"It's not the first time I've been glad," retorted Marilla. "You do like to rub things in, Matthew Cuthbert."

Anne went home to Avonlea with Matthew and Marilla that evening. The apple blossoms were out and the world was fresh and young. Diana was at Green Gables to meet her. In her own white room, where Marilla had set a flowering house rose on the window sill, Anne looked about her and drew a long breath of happiness.

Part VI

The Bend in the Road

WHEN ANNE CAME home that day for the summer she realized that Matthew was not looking well. Marilla then explained that Matthew had had some bad spells with his heart that spring. "I'm real worried about him, but he's some bit better now and we've got a good hired man, so I'm hoping he'll kind of rest and pick up. Maybe he will now you're home. You always cheer him up."

"You are not looking well yourself as I'd like to see you, Marilla," said Anne. "You look tired. I'm afraid you've been working too hard. You must take a rest, now that I'm home."

"It's not the work—it's my eyes. I can't read or sew with any comfort now. I'll have to see the eye doctor soon when he comes."

That evening Anne went out with Matthew to get the cows. Matthew walked slowly with bent head.

"You've been working too hard today, Matthew," said Anne. "Why won't you take things easier?"

*That evening Anne went out with Matthew
to get the cows.*

"Well now, I can't seem to," said Matthew. "It's only that I'm getting old, Anne, and keep forgetting it."

"If I had been the boy you sent for," said Anne, "I'd be able to help you so much now and spare you in a hundred ways."

"Well now, I'd rather have you than a dozen boys, Anne," said Matthew patting her hand. "Just mind you that—rather than a dozen boys. Well now, I guess it wasn't a boy that took the Avery scholarship, was it? It was a girl—my girl—my girl that I'm proud of."

He smiled his shy smile at her as he went into the yard. Anne took the memory of it with her when she went to her room that night and sat for a long while at her open window, thinking of the past and dreaming of the future.

The next morning Matthew was standing in the kitchen doorway, a folded paper in his hand, his face strangely gray, when he fell over in a faint. The hired man, who had just come with the mail, rode off for the doctor. Before the doctor could arrive, Rachel Lynde came and saw at once that Matthew was dead. The doctor later said that the death had come by some sudden shock. The secret was discovered in the paper Matthew had held. All his money had disappeared with the failing of the local bank.

At the funeral Anne could not cry. It seemed to her a terrible thing that she could not shed a tear for Matthew, whom she had loved so much and who had been so kind to her, Matthew, who had walked with her last evening at sunset and was now lying in the dim room below. But no tears came at first.

In the night she woke up, with the stillness and the darkness about her, and she could see in her memory Matthew's face smiling at her as he had smiled when they parted at the gate that last evening—she could hear his voice saying, "My girl—my girl that I'm proud of." Then the tears came and Anne wept her heart out.

Marilla heard her and crept in to comfort her.

"Oh, Marilla, what will we do without him?"

"We've got each other, Anne. I don't know what I'd do if you weren't here—if you'd never come. Oh, Anne, I know I've been kind of strict and harsh with you maybe—but you mustn't think I didn't love you as well as Matthew did. I want to tell you now when I can. It's never been easy for me to say things out of my heart, but at times like this it's easier. I love you as dear as if you were my own flesh and blood and you've been my joy and comfort ever since you came to Green Gables."

Days later, Marilla saw the eye specialist.

"What did he say?" asked Anne.

"He examined my eyes. He says that if I give up all reading and sewing entirely and any kind of work that strains the eyes, he thinks my eyes may not get any worse and my headaches will be cured. But if I don't he says I'll certainly be stone blind in six months. Blind! Anne, just think of it! What am I to live for if I can't read or sew or do anything like that? I might as well be blind—or dead."

When Marilla had eaten her supper Anne persuaded her to go to bed. Then Anne went herself to her room and sat down by her window in the darkness with her tears and a heavy heart. How sadly things had changed since she had sat there the night after coming home!

One afternoon a few days later Marilla met with a man who had come out from town.

"What did Mr. Sadler want, Marilla?" asked Anne.

"He heard that I was going to sell Green Gables and he wants to buy it."

"Buy it! Buy Green Gables? Oh, Marilla, you don't mean to sell Green Gables?"

"Anne, I don't know what else is to be done. I've thought it all over. If my eyes were strong I could stay here and make out to look after things and manage, with a good hired man. But as it is, I can't. I may lose my sight; and anyway I'll not be fit to run things. Oh, I never thought I'd live to see the day when I'd have to sell my home. I'm thankful you're provided for with that scholarship, Anne. I'm sorry you won't have a home to come to on your vacations, that's all, but I suppose you'll manage somehow." Marilla broke down and wept.

"You mustn't sell Green Gables," said Anne. "You won't have to stay here alone. I'm not going to Redmond College."

"Not going to Redmond! Why, what do you mean?"

"Just what I say. I'm not going to take the scholarship. You surely don't think I could leave you alone in your trouble, Marilla, after all you've done for me. Mr. Barry wants to rent the farm for next year. So you won't have any bother over that. And I'm going to teach. I've applied for the school here—but I don't expect to get it for I understand the trustees have promised it to Gilbert Blythe. But I can have the Carmody school—Mr. Blair told me so last night at the store. Oh, I have it all planned out, Marilla. And I'll read to you and keep you cheered up. You won't be bored or lonesome. And we'll be real cozy and happy here together, you and I."

"Oh, Anne, I could get on real well if you were here, I know. But I can't let you sacrifice yourself so for me. It would be terrible."

"Nonsense! There is no sacrifice. Nothing could be worse than giving up Green Gables— nothing could hurt me more. We must keep the dear old place. My mind is quite made up, Marilla. I'm not going to Redmond; and I *am* going to stay here and teach. Don't you worry about me a bit. I'm heart glad over the very thought of staying at dear Green Gables. Nobody could love it as you and I do—so we must keep it."

"You blessed girl!" said Marilla. "I feel as if you'd given me new life. I guess I ought to stick out and make you go to college—but I know I can't, so I ain't going to try, Anne."

When it became noised abroad in Avonlea that Anne Shirley had given up the idea of going to college and intended to stay home and teach there was a good deal of discussion over it. Most of the good folks, not knowing about Marilla's eyes, thought she was foolish. Mrs. Lynde did not. She came up one evening and found Anne and Marilla sitting at the front door in the warm, scented summer dusk.

Mrs. Rachel deposited her substantial person upon the stone bench by the door, behind which grew a row of tall pink and yellow hollyhocks, with a long breath of mingled weariness and relief.

"Well, Anne, I hear you've given up your notion of going to college. I was real glad to hear it. You've got as much education now as a woman can be comfortable with. I don't believe in girls going to college with the men and cramming their heads full of Latin and Greek and all that nonsense."

"But I'm going to study Latin and Greek just the same, Mrs. Lynde," said Anne laughing. "I'm going to take my Arts course right here at Green Gables, and study everything that I would at college."

Mrs. Lynde lifted her hands in holy horror.

"Anne Shirley, you'll kill yourself."

"Not a bit of it. I shall thrive on it. Oh, I'm not going to overdo things. But I'll have lots of spare time in the long winter evenings. I'm going to teach over at Carmody, you know."

"I don't know it. I guess you're going to teach right here in Avonlea. The trustees have decided to give you the school."

"Mrs. Lynde!" cried Anne, springing to her feet in her surprise. "Why, I thought they had promised it to Gilbert Blythe!"

"So they did. But as soon as Gilbert heard that you had applied for it he went to them and told them that he withdrew his application, and suggested that they accept yours. He said he was going to teach at White Sands. Of course he gave up the school just to oblige you, and I must say I think it was real kind and thoughtful in him, that's what."

After Mrs. Lynde left, Anne went to the little Avonlea graveyard to put fresh flowers on Matthew's grave and water the Scotch rosebush. She lingered there until dusk, liking the peace and calm of the little place.

On her way home, Anne saw a tall lad come whistling out of a gate before the Blythe homestead. It was Gilbert, and the whistle died on his lips as he recognized Anne. He lifted his cap courteously, but he would have passed on in silence, if Anne had not stopped and held out her hand.

"Gilbert," she said, with scarlet cheeks, "I want to thank you for giving up the school for me. It was very good of you—and I want you to know that I appreciate it."

Gilbert took the offered hand eagerly.

"It wasn't particularly good of me at all, Anne. I was pleased to be able to do you some small service. Are we going to be friends after this? Have you really forgiven me my old fault?"

Anne laughed and tried unsuccessfully to withdraw her hand.

"I forgave you that day by the pond landing, although I didn't know it. What a stubborn little goose I was. I've been—I may as well make a complete confession—I've been sorry ever since."

"We are going to be the best of friends," said Gilbert, jubilantly. "We were born to be good friends, Anne. You've thwarted destiny long enough. I know we can help each other in many ways. You are going to keep up your studies, aren't you? So am I. Come, I'm going to walk home with you."

That night Anne sat long at her window. The wind purred in the cherry tree. The stars twinkled over the trees.

Anne's horizons had closed in since the night she had sat there after coming home from Queen's Academy. But the joys of sincere work and friendship were to be hers; and, besides, nothing could rob her of her imagination. There was always the bend in the road! And who knew what lay on the other side of that bend?

"'God's in his heaven, all's right with the world,'" whispered Anne softly.